My l
Calling All Piglets

9/10

Calling All Piglets!

3 1389 01984 4398

A Level 1 Early Reader

Copyright © 2008 Disney Enterprises, Inc.
All Rights Reserved. Based on the *Winnie the Pooh* works, by A.A. Milne and E.H. Shepard
Published by Dalmatian Press, LLC, in conjunction with Disney Enterprises, Inc.

08 09 10 NGS 10 9 8 7 6 5 4 3 2 1
17588 Disney My Friends Tigger & Pooh Early Reader - Calling All Piglets!

One day, Piglet was
at his house.
It was a fall day.

"It is a good fall day," said Piglet.
"I like the wind.
 I like the wind in the Wood.
 I will go to the Wood."

Flap, flap, flap.

"What is that?" said Piglet.

Flap, flap, flap.

He looked and looked.

He saw something pink.

He saw something pink—flapping!

"It looks like me!" said Piglet.
"But I am Piglet.
Two Piglets!
How can that be?"

Piglet ran and ran!

He hid at a big rock.

Oh, no!

He saw something pink!

"Three Piglets!" said Piglet.

"How can that be?"

He ran and ran and ran!

He hid up a tall tree.

Oh, no!

He saw something pink!

"Four Piglets!" he said.

"How can that be?"

Piglet ran and ran.
"I will call
for help,"
he said.

SSuuuUUpppperrrr sslllEEEUUtthhs!

Piglet called the Super Sleuths,
Pooh, Darby, Tigger, and Buster.
"Time to slap my cap!" said Darby.

The Super Sleuths saw the flag.

The flag had Piglet's house.

"We will help you, Piglet!" called Pooh.

"Any time, any place,
The Super Sleuths are on the case!"

"I saw three Piglets!" said Piglet.
"Three Piglets in pink!"

"Think, think, think,"
said Darby.
"Three Piglets in pink.
How can that be?"

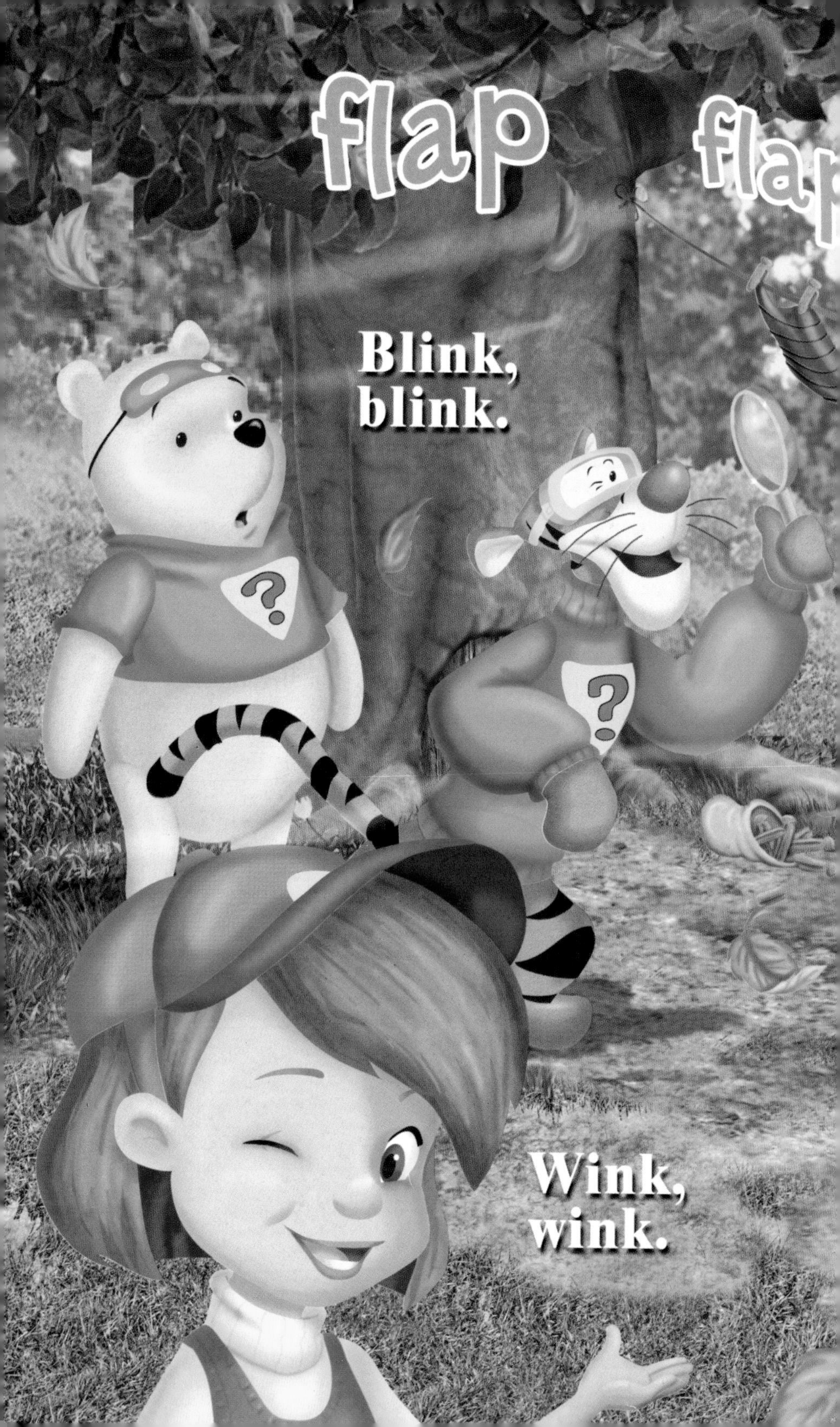

Blink,
blink.

Wink,
wink.

flap flap

SERS

"I see a lot of pink, too," Darby said.
"Think, Piglet. Where did you see
  the pink?"
"In the Wood," said Piglet. "Come on!"

Piglet took all the
Super Sleuths to the Wood.
"Calling all Piglets!"
called Darby.

"Aha! Yes!" said Tigger.
"I see something pink!"

"Hmmm…" said Pooh.
"I see something pink!"

"Look!" said Darby.
"I see something pink!"

"Oh, my," said Piglet.
"Three pink tops. The tops are
   off the three Piglets!"

Darby hugged Piglet.
"No," she said. "All the tops are
your tops. At your house,
the big wind shook your tops..."

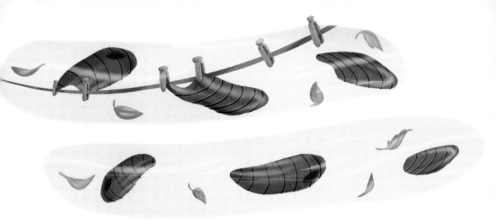

"And took
your tops,"
said Tigger.

"And, look!
Your tops are
in the Wood!"
said Pooh.

"Oh," said Piglet.
"It was the big wind.
It was not three Piglets."

"I like one Piglet.
    One Piglet is good," said Pooh.
"Thank you, Pooh," said Piglet.